MEET THE GIRL TALK CHARACTERS

Sabrina Wells is petite, with curly auburn hair, sparkling hazel eyes, and a bubbly personality. Sabrina loves magazines, shopping, sleepovers, and most of all, she loves talking to her best friends.

Katie Campbell is a straight-A student and super athlete. With her blond hair, blue eyes, and matching clothes, she's everyone's idea of little miss perfect. But Katie has a few surprises for everyone, including herself!

Randy Zak has just moved to Acorn Falls from New York City, and is she ever cool! With her radical spiked haircut and her hip New York clothes, Randy teaches everyone just how much fun it is to be different.

Allison Cloud is a Native American Indian. Allison's super smart and really beautiful. But she has one major problem: She's thirteen years old, five foot seven, and still growing!

Here's what they're talking about in
Girl Talk

ALLISON: Hi, Randy. Your show was great tonight. I love the music and I love all that cool advice you're giving people over the air.

RANDY: Thanks Al, but I think this whole D.J. thing has gotten out of hand.

ALLISON: Are you kidding! All the kids in Acorn Falls love your radio show, and everyone is dying to find out about the mystery D.J.!

RANDY: Well, I happened to tell one guy to watch his girlfriend, and it just *happened* to be true, and now every time I'm on the air people want advice.

ALLISON: Well, get ready because I heard that even Stacy the great is planning on giving you a call!

ON THE AIR

By L. E. Blair

GIRL TALK® series created by Western Publishing Company, Inc.

Produced by Angel Entertainment, Inc.

Western Publishing Company, Inc., Racine, Wisconsin 53404

Text by Lea Jerome

Chapter One

"Hey, Randy, did you hear Spike's show last night on KTOP 1350?" Sabrina asked as she walked up behind me at my locker. "It was awesome. He played two straight hours of surfing music."

I grabbed my lunch off the top shelf of my locker and turned to face Sabrina Wells, who is one of my best friends. "Hi, Sabs," I said, kicking my locker shut behind me. "Of course I heard Spike's show. I never miss it. Are you heading to lunch? We'd better hurry or we'll never get a table."

Sabs continued talking about Spike's show as we headed to the lunchroom. I admit I wasn't paying much attention to her. I just couldn't stop thinking about the radio broadcasting class I was taking once a week on Monday nights. I was trying to learn about being a D.J. I had gone to a class the night before, and our assignment for the coming week was to plan out an hour-long radio show.

It happens to involve split-second timing to play music, talk on the air, and still do commercial breaks and station identification at just the right times. The whole process is a lot more complicated than most people think. It's pretty cool stuff, though, especially for someone who's totally into music, the way I am.

"Hey, Randy, did you hear what I just said?" asked Sabs, poking my arm.

"Sorry, Sabs, I guess I was preoccupied," I said, really looking at her this time. She's a couple of inches shorter than I am, with long, curly red hair and tons of energy.

"Well, do you think Spike's going to be a professional D.J. or anything? He's really good," Sabs asked me again.

Spike lives down the street from me. He was the first person I met in Acorn Falls, Minnesota, when I moved here with my mom from New York City last summer, after she and my dad got divorced. Spike is totally cool, and he's in ninth grade. I'm only in seventh, so we go to different schools.

Anyway, he's a D.J. at Bradley High's radio station, KTOP at 1350 on the AM dial, which also happens to be where I'm taking my radio broadcasting class. Spike plays lead guitar in this really cool band called Wide Awake, too. The guy totally lives, sleeps, and breathes music.

"I don't know, Sabs," I said, answering her question. "Spike's not the kind of person who would think about being a D.J. as a career or anything. He just likes playing music, but I was really surprised that he put on that much surfing music last night, though."

Not that Spike hates beach tunes or anything. I just didn't think they were at the top of his list of favorites. I couldn't help thinking that if I had been planning his show, I would have played some music that was a bit more radical.

Sabs giggled. "Well, Arizonna called Spike up last night and requested some Beach Boys."

"Arizonna, huh? It figures," I said, grinning. Arizonna is pretty new at Bradley Junior High. He's from Los Angeles, and he's a total surfer dude. Actually, I think he's really cool. He's different from anyone here in Acorn Falls. I can respect that. Some people think I'm kind of different, too, since I grew up in New York City.

"How do you know Arizonna called Spike?" I asked Sabs.

Sabs brushed her curly hair back over her shoulder and replied, "He called from my house. He was studying with Sam and me." She tried to say it matter-of-factly, but she was turning beet-red again. Sabs blushes more than anyone I have ever met, especially when it comes to guys she has a crush on.

I could tell that we were getting closer to the cafeteria — the noise level was definitely rising. Sabs and I got our lunches and went in search of a table.

"Hey, there's Allison!" Sabs exclaimed, while pointing to a table in the back. Allison Cloud is another of my best friends. She is one hundred percent Chippewa Indian, and she knows me better than anyone else on the planet — except for my mom and Sheck, my best friend back in New York City.

Allison looked up from her book as I sat down on the chair opposite her. "Hi, Al," I said, opening my lunch bag and pulling out my yogurt and a cheese and alfalfa sprout sandwich. "How's it going?"

She smiled and put down her book. Al is really tall, and she has long dark hair and these big brown eyes. She reads all the time, and I mean all the time. Once I even caught her with a book open while she was on her way home from school, reading as she went. Al told me that she read over one hundred books last summer, just to see if she could do it. I hope she had her library card laminated — it was probably just about shredded from all that use.

"You guys, do you think Arizonna had anything to do with all that surfing music on Spike's show last night?" Katie Campbell asked, putting her lunch tray on the table as she appeared next to me. Katie is our other best friend.

My mother tells me I've really grown since we moved here, and I guess the fact that Katie and I are friends proves that she's right. If we still lived in New York and I met Katie, I'd probably just think she was a major prep. She has long blond hair, blue eyes, and dimples, and she is really into wearing things like pastels and coordinated headbands and argyle socks. Actually, Katie's a really interesting person. I flipped when she quit the flag team and joined the boys' ice hockey team earlier this year. It's not exactly the perfect prep thing to do.

"What are you talking about?" Sabs asked, trying to look innocent and not having much success. Her face shows every emotion. "Okay, okay," she said, giggling. "You're right, it was all Arizonna's fault. He requested it."

A second later, I heard a gushing, obnoxious voice behind me say, "Did you hear Spike's show last night? He's so cool."

I swiveled in my chair to see Stacy the Great Hansen and her band of followers sitting at the next table. Stacy is not my favorite person. It probably has a lot to do with the fact that she thinks she is queen of the school, or something, just because her father is principal of the school.

"That music he played last night was really great. Definitely on the cutting edge," Stacy went on, flipping her long blond hair over her shoulder. I started to ask Stacy just what she knew about the cutting edge of anything, but I caught myself. Talking to someone like her just wasn't worth the energy.

I turned back to my friends and rolled my

eyes. Sabs, Katie, and Allison all giggled. They feel the same way about Stacy as I do.

"So," Arizonna said, walking up to our table, turning toward us. "What's up?"

"Hey, Zone," I replied, scooping up the last of my yogurt. I don't remember when I started calling Arizonna that, but now I never even think of using his real name. "Do you want to go skateboarding today?"

"Most assuredly," he said, brushing his long blond bangs out of his eyes. Arizonna has this straight light blond hair that always falls into his face, and he's still a little tanned from when he lived in L.A. "You know, R.Z., I didn't think I would ever get into this skateboard thing. I mean, it isn't connected to nature the way surfing is — just you, your board, and the ocean out there. Skateboarding seemed so earth-bound."

"I thought you liked skateboarding," Sabs put in, sounding confused.

"I do," Arizonna told her. "But it's really different. My buddies in L.A. would be in total shock if they knew that I'm into wheels and concrete now."

"Hey, Arizonna," a boy's voice called from a

7

few tables away. I looked over and saw Sam, Sabs's twin brother, getting up from where he was sitting with his two best friends, Nick Robbins and Jason McKee. He came over to our table and bumped fists with Arizonna.

"Let me guess," Sam said. "You requested all those surfing tunes last night?"

"Wasn't it awesome?" Arizonna asked. "I'm psyched that there's alternative radio here. KTOP saved my life."

"I know what you mean," I agreed. I kind of felt the same way. When I first moved here, everything was so different. I was used to the hectic pace of New York City, where there is always something new to see and all these different types of music on the radio. When I got to Acorn Falls, it seemed as if every station played the same kind of music — pop. All the songs had the same beat. I guess I notice things like that because I'm a drummer.

But KTOP 1350 is totally different. It plays reggae, classical, opera, folk, jazz, new wave, New Age. You name it. It's like all the different radio stations of New York rolled into one. The high school students run the station, which I think is really great. That's one of the reasons I decided to take the broadcasting class there, so I can D.J. at KTOP when I get to ninth grade.

"How's your radio broadcasting class, Randy?" Allison asked me as Sam and Arizonna continued talking. "What did you do last night?"

Leave it to Al to guess exactly what's on my mind. She must have known that all this talk about KTOP was making me think about my class.

"Oh, my gosh, that's right!" Sabs exclaimed. "The class is almost over, isn't it? You must be so excited. Pretty soon you can be a D.J., too."

I nodded and explained, "Next Monday is the last class. It's been really cool." I told them all about the rap show I had planned out. "Even on KTOP they don't play a lot of rap, so I thought it would make a good theme," I began.

"It sounds really interesting," Al commented. "Does the rest of the class like the idea?"

I couldn't help grinning. "C.J. said it would be good enough for his show," I told my friends. C. J. Pratt is a D.J. for a Minneapolis station that plays pretty cool music. He drives all the way to Acorn Falls every week just to teach the class.

"That's great!" Katie exclaimed. "You should be really proud."

I guess I was proud. It was funny, but every time I listened to the radio now, I thought of how I would do a show if I were the D.J. I mean, I do know a lot about music. And I couldn't help imagining what it would be like to actually go on the air. Not to be dramatic or anything, but sometimes I think I'd do absolutely anything for the chance to work on a real radio station.

Chapter Two

When I got home from school later that afternoon, the phone rang as I walked in the door. I flew toward the kitchen to grab it.

"Hi, Ran. Listen, do you want to help me out tonight?"

It was Spike. I sat down on this old step stool we have in the corner of the kitchen — if you can call it a kitchen. I mean, it has all the appliances and everything, but it isn't a separate room. I live in a converted barn. It's really just one big room, except for M's room, which is screened off, and my bedroom, which is upstairs in the loft. The bathroom is the only room in the house that really has a door.

"Help you do what?" I asked, opening the refrigerator door. I figured I should start thinking about dinner. I knew without having to look that M was wrapped up in her studio at the back of the barn. She's an artist. She also happens to be my mother, and I know from experience that when she's in a creating mood, she forgets to do normal stuff — like eat and sleep.

When we first moved here, she was in this painting phase, mostly still lifes. Then she got into papier-mâché sculpture. That was wild. Now she's into life forms, and she does mostly charcoal drawings and watercolors. M says that motion is what interests her, so she has to use a medium that flows. Whenever I use watercolors, they run and drip more than they flow. But I'm not the one with the one-person show coming up in Minneapolis, so what do I know?

"Help me at the station," Spike explained. "You know Mikki, my assistant? Her grandmother is sick and she's going to be away for at least two weeks! Ran, you have to help me. You'll be home by nine o'clock, I promise."

"You want me to help on KTOP?" I asked, feeling a little shocked. I don't know why, but it was about the last thing I would have expected Spike to say.

I could hear Spike laugh over the line. "That's what I said. Now, are you up for it, or aren't you?"

I didn't hesitate at all. "Yes! Definitely!" This was so cool! It was exactly what I had been hoping for. Spike let Mikki talk on the air and everything. "Let me just check with M," I said into the receiver, jumping up from the step stool.

"Listen, I've got to run," Spike said. "Call me back if there's a problem. If not, I'll swing by and get you at a quarter to six."

After I hung up, I pulled some whole wheat pizza dough out of the freezer, then went back to M's studio. M said it was cool with her if I helped Spike, as long as I got my homework done before I left.

I knew my friends were going to flip when they found out, but I was so busy making dinner and doing my homework that I didn't have a second to call them and tell them to listen to KTOP 1350. Then Spike showed up early, and I didn't want to ask him to wait.

I have to say that in addition to being a good friend, Spike is a very cool-looking guy. He has this wild brown hair and eyes that are so dark they're almost black. He was wearing black jeans and a T-shirt with a black vest over it. Sabs thinks he looks like Johnny Depp.

It was already dark out as we walked the few blocks over to the high school. It still surprises me how quiet it is here. In New York City there is always a lot of noise. It took me a while to get used to hearing the wind in the trees instead of taxi horns, but now I really like it. It's very calming, as M would say.

"I want to show you around the station first," Spike said when the brick school building came into sight.

I rolled my eyes at him. "Come on, Spike, I already know where everything is from C.J.'s class."

"It's a lot different when you're under pressure, Ran," Spike told me as he headed for the door leading into the new wing of the high school. I was a little annoyed that he was treating me like an amateur. I mean, how different could it be?

Going into the school, we went down a couple of lighted, empty hallways to where the music rooms and the radio station were.

"Yo, Manny, what's up?" Spike said as a teacher in his thirties came out of one of the rooms. I figured he had to be Mr. McManus, the music teacher. Spike had mentioned him to me a couple of times before.

"You're early, Spike," Manny said, pushing up his small, round wire-rimmed glasses. "What's the occasion?"

"This is Randy Zak," Spike replied, gesturing toward me. "She's going to help me out until Mikki comes back."

Mr. McManus looked at me and held out his hand. "How are you, Randy?" he asked. "You don't go to school here, do you? You look kind of familiar, though."

"I go to Bradley Junior High, Mr. McManus," I told him as we shook hands. All of a sudden, I had this sudden paranoid flash that maybe he wouldn't let me help Spike, since I was just in junior high. At that moment it struck me just how much I really wanted to be on the radio. What would I do if Mr. McManus said I couldn't?

"Call me Manny," he replied, grinning at me. "Everyone else does. So where would I know you from?"

He didn't seem at all concerned about my age. I started to relax again. "I play with Iron Wombat," I told him, figuring that maybe he had seen my band at the Battle of the Bands a few months ago.

Manny snapped his fingers. "That's it! You're an excellent drummer," he said. "I'll keep an eye out for you when you get to high school. Your talent would be great for the band."

I didn't think the school band was my kind of scene, but Manny was being so nice to me that I didn't tell him that. He seemed like a really cool teacher, a lot like the teachers in my old school in New York City.

"All right, kids," Manny said, "get to it. I'll be in my office grading papers if you need me."

Spike and I went into the station, which really consisted of a sound studio, a small lounge with a desk, a ratty old couch, and about six chairs scattered around, and the record library.

Through the glass window in one wall of the lounge I could see Smooth-as-Silk, the D.J. who had the five-to-seven spot, doing his show in the soundproofed studio. When he saw Spike and me, Smooth smiled and gave a thumbs-up sign, then continued talking into the microphone in front of him. The red "on the air" light above the studio door was lit.

"What do you want me to do?" I asked

Spike, going over to the studio window and looking inside.

The studio is a really cool place. The desk is set up in a U-shape around the D.J.'s chair, so that everything is easy to reach. Two turntables are on one side of the desk, and a reel-to-reel tape deck and a storage rack of tapes are on the other. There are a couple of phones, too, for listeners to call in to the station and make requests.

I saw that Smooth's records were piled on a special rack right behind the turntables, and his hands were working the audio board in front of him. That's where all the controls are, like volume and the different inputs for the turntables and the tape deck. I had learned how to use the mike and all the controls in my class. Thinking about actually running the board on the air made me feel this rush of adrenaline. I couldn't wait!

"Your job for tonight is mostly going to be answering the phone and pulling the records for requests as they come in," Spike said, coming to stand next to me.

That brought me back down to earth. I should have known that I wouldn't actually be on the air or anything, not on my first night, anyway. I couldn't help feeling a little disappointed. But I didn't want Spike to think that I wasn't grateful, so I smiled and made a salute, saying, "You got it, boss."

I listened as Spike walked me through some of the technical stuff, like signing in the logbook and what to do if there was an emergency announcement, like if there was a tornado or something.

"Not a problem," I told him. After all, he wasn't telling me anything I hadn't already learned in my broadcasting class. "Spike, I've been through all this with C.J. a million times. It's cool."

Then Spike pulled out a piece of paper and handed it to me. "Here's a chart for tonight's show," he said.

The chart was in the shape of a circle. Actually, there were two circles, one for each hour of his show, and they were broken down into different pie-shaped sections for each part of the show — commercials, music, news. Every single second of his show was accounted for. There was even a pie section for the station identification, which only takes about ten seconds. I think that's really incredible. I mean, when you listen to the radio, you're never aware that it's all so precise. Beneath the circles Spike had made a list of the songs he was going to play.

"You can start by getting my records from the record library," he explained, leading the way through a door at the back of the lounge. There were rows and rows of shelves with records on them. "Everything is arranged alphabetically, by category."

He held up his hand, saying, "I know, I know. You already learned this. Sorry, I can't help it." He paused before going back into the lounge. "Oh — you might want to think of a call name for when you answer the phone, too. That way you can remain anonymous." Then he disappeared into the station room.

As I collected Spike's records, I tried to think of what I would call myself. Even though I wouldn't be on the air, I didn't want to use just any name. I wanted something that would make a definite impression.

"Five minutes, Ran!" Spike shouted into the record library after a while.

Five minutes! I felt as if I had just gotten

there. How could all that time be up already? I hadn't even thought of a name to use on the phones yet.

I quickly located the last few records on Spike's list and rushed back to the lounge by the studio. Spike had gone into the studio, I saw, and was talking to Smooth-as-Silk.

"Randy, this is Smooth," Spike said as I walked into the studio and put the stack of albums down on the rack behind the turntables.

I smiled at Smooth, a black guy with razor-cut hair and amber eyes. Seeing that the "on the air" light was on, I raised an eyebrow at Spike. Why were they talking when the show was still on?

"Don't worry. Smooth already wrapped up his show," Spike explained. "The last five minutes of the hour are a news tape, so it's okay to talk until I go on."

"That's right," I said, thinking out loud, "voices in the studio don't go out to radio land unless the mike is on." What an amateur! I was going to have to concentrate more.

"Listen, I'd better go," Smooth said, picking up a huge armful of records from the desk.

"I've got to get all these put away. I'll catch you later."

As Smooth disappeared into the record library, Spike said to me, "I'll help you put our records away at the end. As you can see, there's usually a big pile of them."

I saw that the clock on the wall read four minutes to seven. I sat down on a chair near the phones, while Spike took the D.J.'s chair.

"Ran, do you think you can handle getting the commercial tapes ready, too?" he asked me.

"Not a problem," I replied.

"Great," Spike said. He made a face at the reel-to-reel machine. "That's a dinosaur, since we have to thread the tapes ourselves, but it's all we have. We're trying to save money for a cartridge deck and a CD player, though."

"That would be cool." I went over and threaded the first tape into the machine, remembering to set it so that the commercial would start just a second after the machine was turned on. C.J. calls that "cuing" the tapes. It's very important to do, so that there isn't a lot of "dead air" — that's when there isn't any sound at all going out over the air. Dead air is one of the worst things that can happen in the world of radio — or TV, for that matter.

Spike put on his headphones, then plugged in a second set and handed them to me. "We can listen on these," he told me.

Shooting me a big grin, he added, "It's show time. Let's get to it!" Then he started playing the Grateful Dead song he always used to start his show. It's kind of like his signature.

"I'm ready," I told him. All of this was totally familiar, just like in my classes. What could go wrong?

During the next two hours, I found out that there are really an amazing number of mistakes that are very easy to make in a radio station — and I made all of them. It's funny. Spike's show always seemed so laid back and mellow when I listened to it, but it was totally chaotic in the booth.

First, I was so busy answering the phones that I totally forgot to change the commercial tapes and we were late playing our second commercial. That is a really big mistake, since the tapes have to be played exactly every ten minutes. Since we waited an extra minute, that threw off Spike's whole show.

Needless to say, Spike decided to cue the

next commercial himself. While he was doing that, he asked me to flip the selector on the audio board from turntable one to turntable two. But I switched the selector to the microphone by mistake! There were ten seconds of dead air before Spike figured out what I had done. Ten seconds is a long time to listen to nothing. It was a good thing Spike knew what he was doing, otherwise our poor audience would have been listening to a lot more dead air.

The only good thing that happened was that I came up with a really good call name for myself. I remembered what Stacy had said in the cafeteria that day, about surfing music being on the cutting edge. So now my official name at KTOP was the Cutting Edge. Pretty cool.

Still, by the time the show ended, I was feeling very down and depressed. I hadn't had any clue to what was going on. And I wasn't even doing half the stuff Spike had to handle.

It looked as if my career as a D.J. was going to be a total bomb.

Chapter Three

"Do you mean to say you were helping out on Spike's show last night! I don't believe it!" Sabs exclaimed the next day at lunch.

"That's really great," Katie added, taking a sip of her milk.

I wished I felt as optimistic as my friends did. "You guys, I was totally out of control," I said, explaining all the mistakes I had made the night before.

"Hi, everyone," said Allison, sitting down next to me and taking her sandwich out of her lunch bag. She must have noticed that I was looking bummed out. "What's the matter, Randy?" she asked.

"Randy's upset because she made a couple of mistakes helping out Spike on his show last night," Katie explained.

Allison's brown eyes widened. "You were helping out Spike last night? That's really good news. I'm sure everyone makes mistakes when they're starting out," she told me.

"I don't think you should feel bad about it, Randy," Sabs added. "I was listening to the show, and I hardly even noticed that silence. It was very short."

Sabs is a terrible liar, but it was nice of her to try and make me feel better.

"Face it, you guys," I told my friends. "I bombed. Maybe I should tell Spike to find someone who's better at this stuff than I am."

Sabs, Katie, and Allison all looked at each other. Then Al turned to me and said, "You probably know more than you think you do. What is your class teaching you?"

I took a deep breath. "Well," I began, "we learned about how the timing is really important and you have to plan ahead. . . ."

Thinking about that, I realized that once the show had started, I had totally forgotten about the planning-ahead thing. I had just gotten caught up in the frenzy of the show. "Maybe tonight, if I pay really close attention to the timing, things will go more smoothly," I went on, thinking out loud.

I smiled for the first time all day. Good old

Al. She always comes through by saying just the right thing.

I felt a lot better after that. By the time Spike picked me up at my house that evening, I knew I was ready to do things right. I guess Spike wasn't as convinced as I was, though, because he insisted on picking me up over an hour early again.

"Look, I know I kind of lost control last night," I told him as we were walking to the high school, "but I don't think I need a whole extra hour just to get ready."

Spike just grinned at me. "You definitely are going to need the extra time, Ran," he said, "because I'm going to give you a half hour on the air tonight."

I stopped so suddenly that Spike bumped into me. "What?" I yelped.

"Unless you don't think you're ready to go on the air yet," he went on, shooting me this challenging look.

Even if I hadn't been dying to go on the air, which I definitely was, I can never resist a dare. "I'm ready," I told him, putting my hands on my hips. "I just hope Acorn Falls is ready for my show!"

Half an hour! Great! I could not believe Spike was being so cool after I had gotten so mixed up about things the night before. I even knew exactly what I was going to play. After all, I had just planned out an entire rap show for my class on Monday.

When we arrived at the station, I plunked down on the couch and immediately drew out the chart for my half hour, making sure to account for the commercial and news tapes, and for station identification. Then I filled in the names of rap tunes, leaving space for me to talk over the air, as well as for requests.

I was so busy thinking about my show that I didn't have time to be nervous when Spike switched on his Grateful Dead song to start his show. For the next hour and a half, I remembered to keep my eye on the clock at all times, and I made it through with only a few mistakes. Once I cued up a commercial tape so that there were three seconds of dead air before it started, but Spike assured me that was not a major deal.

Finally Spike got to the bottom of his record pile. He put his last song on, took off his headphones, and turned toward me.

"You're up after this," he said, standing up and gesturing to his seat. "Do you have everything together? Don't worry, Ran, half an hour goes by really fast."

I took a deep breath and cleared my throat. "I'm good to go," I replied. Sitting down, I reached for my first album and put it on the empty turntable, cuing it the way C.J. had shown us.

Spike's last album ended, and he flipped the selector on the board to the microphone setting. "Now we've got a special guest with us for the next two weeks, the one and only Cutting Edge," he announced into the mike. "Tonight I'm giving you a sampling of her Future Shock Show. Let us know what you think."

Future Shock. I liked that. Spike must have made it up on the spur of the moment.

The next thing I knew, Spike was stepping back and pushing the microphone toward me. It was weird, I didn't even think. I just grabbed it and started talking.

"Pump it up out there, y'all," I began. "Are you ready to jam? You've got the Cutting Edge here at KTOP, at 1350 on your AM dial. It's the half hour of power, the Future Shock Show.

Tonight we're going hip-hop and bebop with some major rap tunes. So here's the Rap Master coming at you on turntable one. Pump it up!"

I turned on the turntable and flipped the switch on the audio board to change from the microphone to turntable one. After checking to make sure the volume settings were right, I sat back, breathing deeply.

Spike grinned at me and gave me a thumbs-up. "You might be right, Ran," he said.

"About what?" I asked, reaching for my second album and putting it on turntable two. My mind was already jumping ahead to what I would say next.

"Acorn Falls might not be ready for this," he said, laughing. "But it's hot. I think you were born for this!"

Maybe that was a slight exaggeration, but I was loving every second. I grinned back at Spike and reached for the mike as the rap came to a close. "Party people, let me hear you say yeah!" I began. "Pick up the phone and give me a call. Get your requests in here and let me know how you want to rap. The Edge is on KTOP tonight, and 1350 will never be the same again. Here's rap number two coming at you."

I had just started up turntable two when the phone started ringing. "1350," Spike said, picking up the receiver. "You want the Edge? Please hold." He grinned at me. "You might want to put some of these on the air. Everyone loves that. It's great advertising."

Checking my chart, I saw that there was some time before my first commercial tape. So after my second rap song ended, I flipped the switch on the board to the telephone setting, then grabbed the receiver from Spike.

"You've got the Edge," I said into the phone.

I expected to hear someone's voice, but instead there was this loud screeching noise. I looked at Spike in alarm, and he mouthed the word *feedback* to me. I had forgotten about feedback! It happens sometimes if the person who calls in has their radio on in the background.

"Can you turn your radio off?" I told the person. A second later, the screeching stopped, and a guy's voice asked, "Hello, is this the Cutting Edge?"

I rolled my eyes at Spike. I had just said I was the Edge. He grinned at me and shrugged. C.J. had warned us that this would happen.

"You've got her. What can I do for you?"

"Edge, the turntable is sizzling tonight!" the guy said.

Suddenly I forgave him for asking me who I was after I had already told him. My first fan! "Thanks," I said quickly. "Who's rapping at me?"

"This is Mike," the guy answered.

"Mike, you're on the mike," I told him. "Do you want to say anything to the party people out there?"

After a short pause, Mike said, "Actually, I'm calling because I'm kind of upset about my girlfriend. I think she might be dating someone else."

"What makes you think that, Mike?" I asked.

"Some of her friends were teasing her about this other guy," he replied.

"And you got mad?" I wanted to know.

"You bet!" Mike exclaimed, laughing. "I was out of my mind!"

"Yo, Mike!" I said. "Did she say he was just a friend?"

Mike sounded surprised as he asked, "How'd you know that? Do I know you?"

"Most certainly not," I told him. "It's a woman's intuition." I quickly shuffled through my stack of records and pulled one out. Holding the phone between my shoulder and chin, I dropped the disc on the turntable and cued it as I talked.

"Listen up, Mike. This next tune is for you. Your girl may think the guy is only a friend, but what does the other guy think? Check out the rap!"

I turned off the mike and sat back just as the phone rang again. Spike picked it up. "1350," he said. "You've got the Future Shock Show."

After a pause, he nodded. "Okay, the Cutting Edge will try to get to that. Thanks for calling." He hung up and told me the name of the song the person had requested. "Do I have to dig up the album?"

"Got it right here, Spike," I replied, grinning at him as I pulled it out of my pile.

"Hey, I like working for you," Spike replied, laughing. "I'll just put my feet up and relax."

Looking at the clock, I saw that it was almost time for my first commercial tape. "Am I doing all right?" I asked Spike as I reached for the reel and started threading it into the tape deck.

All of a sudden, I wanted a little reassurance. I mean, I was having a great time, but I didn't think that was the same thing as being good.

Spike shrugged. "I guess you'll do," he teased.

I threw a pen at him.

"No, but seriously, Ran, you've had two phone calls already," Spike said. "That's major. You're on your way to becoming a star."

I smiled at him. "Well, I'll try to remember who gave me my big break when I hit national radio," I joked.

"You'd better," Spike warned. "And remember, the name's Spike. S-P-I-K-E. I took a little unknown junior high kid and molded her into the voice of young America — the D.J. of the future."

I threw another pen at him.

"Hey, hey," he said, holding up his hands. "I give up, but you're going to have dead air soon if you don't flip to your commercial."

I gasped and whirled around in my chair, turning on the tape deck just in time and hitting the right switch on the audio board.

After the ad tape, I couldn't believe how fast the rest of the show went. Spike was totally right, that half hour just whizzed by. It was hard to say "See ya!" at the end of the show. I wanted to stay there all night. Spike said I could keep doing the show until Mikki came back.

Awesome. I couldn't wait for tomorrow night's Future Shock Show!

Chapter Four

"What did you guys think of the Future Shock Show last night?" I asked Sabs and Katie the next morning in homeroom.

I couldn't wait to find out if they had liked Future Shock. I was sure they would have listened to it, since they knew I was helping Spike. By the time I'd gotten home and talked to M about the show the night before, it was too late for me to call anyone, so this was the first chance I'd had to talk to my friends.

Sabs and Katie looked at each other, and Katie began fumbling for something in her book bag.

"Um, I didn't really get a chance to listen, Randy," Sabs said, "My homework took longer than I expected."

What was going on here? Since when would Sabs miss Spike's show to do her homework?

"Katie, did you hear the show?" I pressed,

looking at Kate.

Katie finally looked at me and said, "I went shopping with my mom and we got home kind of late, sorry. Was it good?"

"You missed the show!" I think I was screaming but I couldn't help it. I couldn't believe my best friends missed my big debut.

Sabs and Katie looked at each other. Then they burst out laughing.

"Of course we heard the show!" they squealed at the same time.

"We were just teasing you, Randy. It was a *really* wild show last night," Katie said. "I loved it."

Sabs giggled. "You're a major celebrity. Everyone was listening to you last night, Randy. You were great."

I was really happy they had liked the show. "I'm just an amateur. It was probably just beginner's luck, or something."

"You know it wasn't just beginner's luck," Katie said.

I grinned. "Yeah, I guess I do," I admitted.

We all laughed. Sometimes I have a problem with confidence but, if I'm good at something, I can usually admit it to myself. Not that I brag, or anything.

Just as the final bell rang, Allison slipped into class and sat down at her desk behind Katie.

"Did you listen to Spike's show on KTOP last night?" Sabs asked her, looking as if she was going to burst.

"Yes," Allison replied. She swiveled around and smiled at me. "Randy, I really liked your Future Shock Show. It was very different."

I grinned at her. "I'm glad you liked it."

Al nodded. "You were great. And you sounded totally in control. I just knew you could do it."

The loudspeaker suddenly crackled to life, so Sabs and I rushed across the room to our seats. As Mr. Hansen began morning announcements, I tuned him out a little. I never really listen to him, anyway. If the principal says anything important, one of my friends always lets me know what was said.

I have to admit, I didn't pay much attention in English, either. I mean, I usually like English. Ms. Staats, our teacher, makes things really interesting. But I couldn't get my mind off my next Future Shock radio show.

I had to think of a different music theme for tonight. I didn't want to play rap again, at least not so soon.

"I can't believe Mr. Hansen is thinking about instituting a dress code!" Katie exclaimed as she, Sabs, Al, and I walked into the hallway after class ended.

"That's so lame," Sabs agreed.

I looked at my friends, feeling confused. "What are you guys talking about?" I asked. A dress code? That was absurd.

"Mr. Hansen and the school board think that they might start a dress code here at Bradley," Katie explained as we reached the locker she shares with Sabs.

We all stopped while Katie spun the combination lock. Opening the locker door, Katie paused when it was slightly ajar and then stepped quickly back as she pulled it all the way open. A pile of books fell onto the floor.

"You're getting really good at that," Sabs said, laughing as she bent to retrieve the books and toss them back into the locker. "You almost never get hit by flying textbooks anymore."

Katie grinned at her locker mate. "I've given up trying to keep your part of the locker neat, too," she said. "Sharing a locker with you is really an adventure, Sabs."

"You sound just like my mother when she talks about my room at home," Sabs replied, rolling her eyes. "Just don't start telling me this locker looks like a tornado hit it!"

I laughed. That definitely sounded like something Mrs. Wells would say. But then I got serious. This dress code thing had me worried.

"So what else did Mr. Hansen say about the dress code?" I asked after Katie and Sabs had put their books in their lockers and we headed for the cafeteria for lunch.

"He said he was worried about extreme styles and sloppiness," Sabs told me. She shrugged, adding, "I guess that kinda makes sense."

I looked at her in surprise. "But, Sabs, you don't want someone telling you what you can and can't wear, do you?" I asked.

"He doesn't mean us, Randy," Sabs said, laughing. "We definitely don't dress sloppy. But I guess I am worried about the shorts thing."

"What shorts thing?" I asked. I was starting to feel like a broken record, asking all these questions.

"Don't you ever listen to the announcements?" Sabs asked, grinning at me. She knows full well that I don't, but she just likes to tease me.

"Mr. Hansen wants to ban all shorts in school," Al explained. "But it gets really hot here starting in about May."

"Scorching," Katie agreed. "I'd die if we couldn't wear shorts, especially since Bradley has no air conditioning."

"I'm sweating already just thinking about it," Sabs said, fanning herself. "You don't really think the school board's going to pass the dress code, do you?"

I really hoped not. "I don't think it's fair," I said.

"I agree," Allison put in, nodding. "Students have rights, too."

Al definitely stands up for the things she believes in. She organized a protest a few weeks ago to try to get Bradley to stop using plastic lunch trays that pollute the environment. The protest worked, too! Now the cafeteria uses these cardboard trays that are biodegradable.

"I guess that's true," Sabs said slowly, wrinkling up her nose. "I didn't think of it like that. I just thought Mr. Hansen was worried about ripped jeans and ratty T-shirts."

"There must be something we can do about it!" Katie said as we got on the lunch line. She picked up one of the new cardboard trays and waved it in the air. "After all, Al proved that we can change things at Bradley. It's just that this time we have to show Mr. Hansen that it's important to keep things the same."

Sabs looked uncertainly at Katie, Al, and me. "Do you think the school board's going to listen to us?"

"Maybe we could start a petition," Al suggested. "That would let them know that we're not happy with the dress code."

That was more like it! "Yeah. We could protest at the school board meeting, too," I said.

"But what if that just makes them mad?" Sabs asked. "I wouldn't want the plan to backfire on us."

"Well, they might listen to the president of the class," Allison pointed out, looking at Sabs.

A smile lit up Sabs's face. "Maybe you're

right," she said as we paid for our lunches and found a table. "I could try. Do you think it would work?"

Katie nodded. "You are the representative of the class, after all. Someone's got to speak for us. Who else would they listen to?"

Suddenly I had a totally wild thought, and I laughed out loud.

"What's so funny about all of this?" Sabs asked, looking at me. "I thought you said this was serious."

"It is," I agreed. "But I just thought of something. Do you think people would listen to the Cutting Edge?"

I heard a gasp from Katie, Allison, and Sabs.

"That's a great idea!" Katie exclaimed.

"Definitely," Al agreed, nodding. "And we'll still do the petition and have Sabs talk to the school board, too."

"This is totally awesome," Sabs commented. "But what are you going to say, Randy? I mean, are you just going to talk about how we don't want a dress code?"

"I think it's got to be a little stronger than that," Katie put in. "That's really no different from Sabs going to talk to Mr. Hansen."

"You're right," I agreed. It felt really good to think that as a D.J. I could make a difference about this dress code thing. It was an important responsibility. "We've got to get the whole school involved. A lot of people listen to Spike's show, right?"

Sabs grinned. "Especially now that the Cutting Edge is on it," she said. "Everyone I've talked to heard you last night."

"I even heard Stacy and Eva talking about the Future Shock Show in the hallway before homeroom," Allison added. "They thought the Future Shock Show was neat."

I laughed. "Obviously she doesn't know who the Cutting Edge is," I said. "Hey, you guys, don't tell anyone else, either, okay? Just for a while."

Suddenly I wanted to remain the mysterious Cutting Edge without anyone guessing the truth.

"Okay," Katie agreed. "So what's the Cutting Edge going to do about the dress code?" she asked.

"I don't know yet," I admitted. "But I'll think of something. I've got three more shows this week, then all of next week. Something will come to mind before then."

But as I ate my lunch, no great ideas came to me. I definitely did not want to suggest anything that was going to get me or anyone else in trouble. The last thing we wanted was to make Mr. Hansen angry. Then he would never listen to what we had to say.

I just wanted him to see that the dress code was unfair. The question was, how?

Chapter Five

Unfortunately, not one idea came to me all day. No, that's not true. I had plenty of ideas, but they were all about what kind of music to play on that night's show, not about the dress code. I was still so psyched about getting to D.J. on the air that it was kind of hard to focus on our protest.

M drove me over to the radio station after dinner. I thought about asking her opinion about how to protest the dress code on the radio. But she was busy talking about her gallery show and asking me which pieces I thought she should include, so we never exactly got around to the dress code thing.

"Yo, Randy!" Spike greeted me as I walked into the station. "How's it going?"

"Hey, Spike," I replied, giving him a high five. "It's cool."

"The whole high school was talking about

45

you today," he said, grinning. "You made quite an impression."

I raised an eyebrow and looked at him. "The whole high school?" I asked dubiously. "Don't you think you're exaggerating just a little?"

Spike held up his hands, looking insulted. "It's the truth. After what happened last night, everyone is going to be tuning in to find out what advice you're giving out tonight."

Advice? What was he talking about? "Spike, did I miss something? What happened last night?"

"That guy who was worried about his girlfriend," Spike replied. "It was Mike Lynch, a tenth grader. He and Jenny Boscow broke up last night after the show. It turns out that the Cutting Edge was right all along. Edie was dating another guy at the same time as she and Mike were going out." Spike started cracking up. "Can you believe it? I'm dying!"

I didn't know what he thought was so funny about the whole thing. Suddenly I didn't like the thought that people might call for advice. I mean, if it hadn't been for what I'd told Mike on the air, maybe he and his girlfriend would still be dating.

But then again, maybe that wasn't even true. It seemed pretty hard to believe that Mike and Jenny had really broken up just because of a rap song. Maybe it hadn't had anything to do with me. I was just a voice on the radio. All I wanted was to have a good time, playing music and talking with the audience.

I picked up Spike's record list from the desk in the lounge outside the studio. "I'm off to pull the records. Call me when you go on?"

"Well, if I didn't, what would I play?" Spike asked, brushing his wild brown hair out of his eyes. "You've got all my records."

I laughed. "True, true," I agreed, pushing open the door to the record library. "Catch you in a bit."

Walking up and down the aisles in the library, I realized that I still hadn't thought of anything to say about the dress code. I hoped something would come to me soon.

A minute later, I heard the door to the record library open.

"Well, if it isn't the Cutting Edge," Manny said, coming up behind me. "You've caused quite a stir in Acorn Falls, and you were only on the air for thirty minutes. Unbelievable."

"Thanks," I said.

He smiled, saying, "Are you sure you're not in high school?"

I shook my head. "Bradley Junior High all the way," I told him.

"Well, we'll be waiting when you get here," Manny said, tousling my hair. "You're definitely rough, tough, and ready to rock 'n' roll."

I laughed. It was so weird to hear a teacher in Acorn Falls talking like that.

"Well, good luck tonight," Manny added. "Call me if you need anything." Then he disappeared out the door.

"Ran!" Spike called out, poking his head into the record library. "Moments to air time. Get in gear!"

Luckily, I had pulled all of Spike's records first. I grabbed one last record for my own segment, then hurried back to the studio. The clock read two minutes to seven. Smooth had already left, and the advertising tape that finished out his show was running. Spike was already in the D.J.'s swivel chair, with the headphones on.

I had decided to go with a basic rock 'n' roll

show tonight. It would be a little more main-stream than the rap I'd played the night before. I hoped it would work.

Spike kept me busy again. He got a lot of phone calls, and I was pretty busy running back and forth to the record library for requests. I have to admit I felt pretty good that two people asked when my show was going to be on. Spike said they were my following. What a joker.

Before I knew it, it was already eight-thirty and time for me to go on. I loaded a commercial tape onto the reel-to-reel deck as Spike wrapped up his show.

"Well, people, it's the time you've been waiting for," Spike said into the mike, winking at me. "It's the Future Shock Show, with your fave, the Cutting Edge, right after these commercial messages. Enjoy!"

He flipped the switch on the board to change to the commercial, then took off his headphones and handed them to me.

"Nice intro," I complimented him, patting him on the back. "You're a master."

"Take notes, my pupil," he replied, sitting down next to the phone. "So, what's on Future

Shock tonight?"

I put on the headphones and cued my first two records on turntables one and two. "We're talking major energy. Just sit back and enjoy, teach," I said with a grin.

Just as the commercial ended, I grabbed the mike, hitting the switch for it on the board. "Are you ready to rock the rafters out there in radio land?" I said into the microphone. "You've got the Cutting Edge coming at you, and this is the Future Shock Show on KTOP 1350 AM. Tonight we're going to get down with some rock 'n' roll. Check it out!"

I started up turntable one, flipped the input selector, and checked to make sure that the volume was right. By the time I sat back and looked at Spike, the phone was already ringing.

Spike raised his eyebrows in mock surprise. "Your loyal listeners," he commented, as he picked up the receiver. "1350. Please hold." Then he turned toward me. "It's all yours."

Taking the receiver from him, I said, "You've got the Cutting Edge."

"Edge? This is Nancy," a girl said. "I just wanted you to know this is my absolute favorite song in the world. Thanks for playing it."

"Not a problem," I replied, hanging up the phone. "I like calls like that. No complications, just compliments."

I gasped as I looked over at the turntable. "Oops! Tune's ending," I said quickly. "Don't want dead air." I switched the selector to the microphone just in time. "Rock on, Acorn Falls! You're bad to the bone!" I said just as the phone rang a second time.

I heard Spike saying, "Hold on," and then I saw him gesturing to me and holding out the telephone receiver. I figured that meant he wanted me to take the call on the air, so I flipped the selector and took the receiver from him.

"This is the Future Shock Show, you're on the air," I said.

"Is this the Cutting Edge?" a guy asked.

"You've got her," I replied. "Who's rapping at me?"

"This is Julian," the guy said.

"Julian, what can I do for you? You need a tune?" I asked, pushing my long, spiky bangs out of my face.

"I need a little advice, Edge," Julian continued.

"What's up?" I asked, raising an eyebrow at Spike. After what had happened with Mike and Jenny, I felt kind of uncomfortable about handing out advice. I mean, I was there to spin tunes, not play Ann Landers, right? What is it about radio that makes people call up and ask for advice, anyway? I've never been able to figure that out. I guess it has something to do with the fact that I'm just a voice, and they don't know me and I don't know them.

But Spike just nodded as if it was all on the up and up. I figured I had no choice but to talk to Julian and hope it was something I could handle.

"My folks won't let me have a car, and it's kind of embarrassing," Julian was saying. "I mean, how am I supposed to get around?"

Not a problem, I thought. This was one situation I could definitely handle. Hadn't this guy ever heard of public transportation? "Julian, wake up to the nineties," I said. "It's the decade of conservation. What do you want a car for? Check out alternative methods!"

"What do you mean?" Julian asked, sounding confused. He obviously really wanted that car.

"Pedal power!" I replied, reaching for my next record as I spoke. "Get a bike. Or even cooler, get a board."

There was a long pause. "A board?" Julian finally echoed, sounding as if he wasn't sure what I was talking about.

"Skateboard!" I explained. "Get one. Take it from the Edge, it's the only way to travel."

"A skateboard?" Julian repeated. He was starting to sound like a parrot. "Isn't that for younger kids? I mean, I'm ready for a car!"

I glared at Spike, who was cracking up over by the phones. Obviously this Julian person thought I was a lot older than thirteen years old.

"Would the Edge steer you wrong?" I said firmly into the receiver. "Get a board."

"All right," Julian agreed reluctantly. "Thanks . . . I guess."

"Not a problem," I said, reaching for my next album.

Just as I was about to hang up, Julian said, "Listen, can I request a tune?"

Spike was wearing a second set of headphones, so he could hear every word. Grabbing a pen and notebook, he moved really close to the speaker, playing the dutiful assistant who didn't want to miss a word. I had to cover my mouth to keep from laughing. Spike must get a major rush out of cracking me up. He was always doing it.

"Sure, what's the tune?" I asked.

"I need to hear some Clapton," Julian responded.

"Not a problem," I said. I had already pulled an Eric Clapton album from the record library. I waved it in front of Spike, then put it down on turntable two in place of the record I had already chosen.

"Acorn Falls, let me hear you say yeah! It's time to rock and roll with some serious guitar. I'm the Cutting Edge, and this is the master, Eric Clapton, coming out at you. Keep your dial locked on the Future Shock Show here on KTOP 1350 AM. It can only get hotter!"

As soon as the mike was off and the music started, Spike let out a burst of laughter. "You're uncanny," he said, grinning at me. "How do you know what they're going to request?"

"I guess I must be plugged into the pulse of this neighborhood," I replied, taking the commercial tape he offered me. "Or maybe I'm paying a bunch of people to call in and request things from me just so I can impress you. Did it work?"

"Definitely," Spike said, bending from the waist and making this exaggerated wave with his hand. "I bow to your incredible musical instincts."

I grinned, threading the tape onto the reel-to-reel deck. I definitely felt much more on top of things tonight than I had my first night. I paid particular attention to the clock while I spoke. As the second hand hit the twelve, I flipped the selector to the commercial tape, then pulled the album off the turntable.

I was cuing up my next two records a minute later, when I heard Spike clear his throat. I looked at him, but all he did was point at my microphone.

"What?" I asked him.

"I think your air's kind of fatal," Spike said after a short pause.

"What are you talking about?" I asked, thinking it was some kind of joke.

"Dead air, Edge," Spike said, stifling a laugh. "Dead air."

I gasped and scrambled for the mike. Control? Right! "That few seconds of silence was compliments of the Edge," I said quickly. "Time to catch your breath and gear up for this next tune. Rock on!"

Starting the turntable, I flipped the right switch on the board, then heaved a sigh of relief. Dead air. What an amateur!

"Nice recovery, Ran," Spike said.

Mortified is a word that isn't usually in my vocabulary. But just then that was exactly how I was feeling. "Please, I can't believe I did that!" I exclaimed.

"Don't sweat it," Spike told me. "I'm sure no one really noticed. It was only a few seconds."

It had felt like eternity to me. Still, it was really nice of Spike to try and make me feel better. What a pal. "All right, all right," I said. "But if I get one phone call about that silence . . ."

"Don't worry about it, Ran," Spike said again. "Acorn Falls loves the Cutting Edge. Kids will probably call up and request silences from now on. You've probably started some major trend, or something."

That just reminded me of another thing I felt uneasy about. "Please," I protested. "I'm just a voice on the air. I can't start trends."

Spike shook his head, saying, "Randy, you'd be very surprised at the power a voice on the radio has. Enjoy it while it lasts."

I'd never asked for the power to start trends, I thought as I turned back toward the mike. Now that I was getting the technical side of things under control, I had to start worrying about what I told people over the air.

Then I shook myself. No one was going to do something just because I said to. That was totally ridiculous. Wasn't it?

Chapter Six

I thought Thursday was never going to end. I was totally unprepared for the pop quiz we had in math. And of course gym, which is my last class of the day, seemed as if it went on and on for ever.

I even got hit in the head with the volleyball because I kept thinking about what I was going to do when I went on the air that night. With so many kids at school talking about the Future Shock Show and the Cutting Edge, it was hard to concentrate on volleyball.

Finally the class was over and school was out for the day.

"Hey, R.Z., are you ready to go?"

I turned to see Arizonna coming up next to me in the hallway. He and I had made plans to go to Ted's Skate Shop — that's this little skate-board store on Main Street. I needed new wheels for my board, and Arizonna was thinking about getting a totally new board. He said it was time to upgrade. He'd really gotten into the whole scene, which I thought was great. It was cool to have a friend to go riding around with.

"How'd you get here so quickly, Zone?" I asked him. The bell had just rung about two seconds ago.

"Supersonic transport," he replied, brushing his long blond bangs out of his eyes.

I shot Arizonna a puzzled look. If everyone on the West Coast talks like Zone, I think it's a miracle that the entire state hasn't taken off for outer space. "What?" I asked him.

"I, like, you know, ran," Arizonna explained. "So are you ready to go?"

I couldn't believe what a hurry he was in. Couldn't he see that I didn't even have my skateboard with me? "Let me just dump my books and get my board out of my locker," I said. "Cool your jets."

"We've really got to motor," Arizonna urged.

I stopped in the middle of the crowded hallway, and some guy bumped into me from behind. "What's the deal?" I asked Arizonna. "Something I don't know about?"

"No, it's just that I heard all these dudes are,

like, heading to Ted's today," Arizonna said, pulling me after him down the hall. He was obviously in a major rush.

"What for?" I asked, starting to get annoyed.

"Don't you listen to KTOP 1350?" Zone wanted to know. "I thought you did."

Suddenly I didn't like the way this conversation was heading. Was he talking about my conversation about skateboarding with that guy Julian?

"The Cutting Edge said skateboards were the only way to travel," Arizonna went on to explain. "So all these dudes are going to check it out."

I walked the rest of the way to my locker in silence, tuning Arizonna out. He was telling me all the other words of wisdom the Cutting Edge had dropped on the air last night. Not exactly what I wanted to hear. Why couldn't he have just talked about the music?

Once we got outside, I dropped my skateboard, hopped on, and pushed off down the sidewalk. I immediately felt better being in motion. As I flew down the hill on Oak Street, I could hear Arizonna's board behind me. With the wind in my face, I could almost forget about the whole Future Shock Show.

When we got to Ted's Skate Shop, Arizonna stopped, jumped off his board, and flipped it up with his sneaker, catching it in one hand. He certainly learned fast. I had just taught him that move the week before.

The normally quiet skateboard shop was jumping when we rolled up to the front of the store. I could not believe it. I could see dozens of kids through the storefront window, and some more people were standing outside the entrance.

"Yo, Marco, what's up?" Arizonna asked one of the shop regulars, a dark-haired guy who was leaning against the outside of Ted's, inspecting his board's wheels.

Marco flicked a thumb toward the store. "It's totally nuts in there," he told us. "Don't chance it. It could get ugly."

I just shook my head. "I've got to get new wheels," I said. "These are gone!"

"Mucho luck to you, then, Randy," Marco replied. "If you're not out in a couple of hours, I'll call for the emergency rescue squad."

Arizonna laughed. "Can't be that bad,

dude," he said, hitting fists with Marco.

Despite Marco's warning, I was totally unprepared for the crush of bodies when I opened the door to Ted's. There were kids everywhere!

This was crazy. I had only just mentioned skateboards once on the air. It was a spur-of-the moment kind of suggestion. What was going on?

"Randy!" Ted, the shop owner, called out as I came up to the counter. "Isn't this wild?"

"Wild," I agreed halfheartedly. I mean, I was glad that Ted was doing well. I hang out at the shop a lot, and Ted is definitely one of my friends. He's really young, only like twenty-five, or so. To quote Zone, Ted is a *major* dude.

"I'm going to have to call up the Cutting Edge and offer her a discount or something," Ted went on, not noticing my lack of enthusiasm. "She's great for business!"

"Great," I said, wanting to change the subject. "Listen, Ted, I need some new wheels for my board."

"What color, Randy?" he asked. "No, don't tell me, black, right? Don't you want to try some neon-green or something?"

"Basic black," I said firmly. Ted and I have had this discussion many times before. Ted is really into major neon colors and wild decals for his boards. He can't understand why I stick to plain black for the board and the wheels. I like black. That's all there is to it.

"Where's the Twilight Zone?" Ted asked, looking for Arizonna. "Didn't I see him walk in?"

"He's somewhere," I answered with a wave of my hand. "Zone wants a new board. He says it's time to upgrade."

Ted nodded and winked at me. "I always like a new convert. Looks as if we've got a lot today."

I tried to smile, but I just wanted to get out of this store and back on my skateboard. It really got me bummed out that so many kids were here just because of what I had said.

I paid for my black wheels and turned to go find Arizonna.

"Randy!" Arizonna called out, finding me first. He grabbed my arm excitedly. "I found the most totally happening board. It's so incredible. I almost feel like I caught the perfect wave!"

He was so excited it was hard not to be happy for him, even though now I was going have to stay in this crowded shop even longer.

"Check it out." Arizonna pulled me to the back of the store, where the boards are displayed. If it was possible, I'd have to say that the crowd was even denser back there. Arizonna pointed to a bright neon-green-and-pink- striped board. "What do you think?"

I grinned at him. "It's you, Zone." The colors definitely weren't my style, but it was a bigger, more solid board than the one he had now. "Cool choice."

"Let me give it a test ride." He pulled the board off the shelf and we pushed our way out of the shop.

One good thing about Ted is that he lets his regulars test out a board before buying it. I mean, boards feel a lot different on the road than they do in the shop. It is important to get one that's right for you.

After a few minutes of going up and down the street, Zone announced that he and the pink-and-green-striped board were destined for each other.

I waited outside while Arizonna paid for his board. Nothing could get me back in that store again.

"Hey, we better jam," Zone announced as he dropped his new board on the sidewalk a few minutes later. "I promised Sabs we'd catch her at Fitzie's."

Fitzie's is the hangout for junior high kids in Acorn Falls. It's really great. Fitzie's is almost always packed, and it's a real neighborhood kind of place. Sheck and I never hung out anywhere like it in New York City. I don't even know if there is a place like Fitzie's in New York.

"Let's motor," I agreed, tucking my new wheels in my jacket pocket and hopping on my skateboard.

When we got to Fitzie's, Sabs was one of the first people we saw. She was sitting across from Katie and Allison in a booth near the front. Sam, Jason, Billy, and Nick were sitting in the booth next to them.

"Randy! Arizonna! Over here!" Sabs called, waving to us.

We walked toward them, and Sabs pushed over to make room for us on her bench. Arizonna bumped fists with the guys before we sat down.

"What's up, dudes and babes?" Arizonna

asked, taking a few of Sabs's french fries and munching on them.

Allison and Katie looked up from the vanilla sundae they were sharing. "Hi, Arizonna. Hi, Randy," Al greeted us.

"How was the shop?" Katie asked. "Did you get a new board?"

"Definitely!" Zone exclaimed, holding up his skateboard. "Rad, huh?"

"I love the colors!" Sabs announced.

Arizonna grinned at her. "That's partly why I bought it. Can't be comfortable on an ugly board, right, Randy?"

"You said it," I agreed. The waitress came by, and Arizonna and I ordered sodas. I was parched.

"Man, that store was packed!" Arizonna exclaimed after the waitress left. "Unbelievable! The Cutting Edge definitely made an impact!"

"Great," I mumbled. When would all of this end?

"Really?" Sabs asked, looking at me excitedly. I guess she thought I should be happy I was making such an impact. It wasn't that I didn't want to have an impact. I just didn't want people running around doing whatever I said without even thinking about it.

"What's the matter, Randy?" Jason called over from the guys' booth. "Don't you like the Cutting Edge?"

"I would have thought you would," Sam commented. "She's happening!"

"Yeah," Billy agreed. "Her music pumps!"

"And her rap is plugged in!" Nick added.

I couldn't help smiling. I mean, it was great to hear all my friends telling me how much they liked the Future Shock Show. I had been so preoccupied by seeing all those kids at Ted's that I totally forget that no one else knew I was the Cutting Edge.

"I'm really glad you all like her," Katie told the guys, arching her eyebrows at me. I could tell she was trying not to laugh.

"Like her?" Nick asked. "I want to meet her. We were thinking about heading over to the high school tonight after the show to catch a glimpse. Right, B.D.?" he asked Billy.

I couldn't take it anymore. I was going to have to tell them who the Cutting Edge really was. I mean, they were my friends, too. It wasn't fair to keep them in the dark.

"Listen, guys . . . " I began, but I trailed off as

Sabs, Katie, and Allison all started cracking up.

"What's so funny?" Sam demanded. "We just want to find out who she is. What's the big deal?"

Sabs got enough control over herself to say, "I don't think you've got that far to look. You know the Cutting Edge better than you think." She looked at me with a mischievous twinkle in her eye. "Right, Randy?"

"Randy, what do you know about this?" Zone asked, giving me a suspicious look. "Is there something you girls aren't telling us?"

I just grinned at him.

The next thing I knew, Billy was looking right at me, and there was a glint of understanding in his blue-gray eyes. "Why do I have the funny feeling that the Cutting Edge is about to be unmasked?" he asked slowly. "And she just happens to be sitting right there at your table."

I could see why Billy and Allison are such good friends. Allison's got this sixth sense about people and situations sometimes. I think Billy's got it, too. Or maybe she's just rubbing off on him.

"What!" Sam and Nick exclaimed at the

same time.

Arizonna hit his forehead lightly with the palm of his hand. "Don't tell me!" he said, groaning. "Randy, why didn't you tell me?"

"Randy?" Jason asked in confusion. "Oh, no! I don't believe it!"

What a goof! I have to admit I was kind of enjoying the whole thing. "Believe it," I told them. "I'm the Cutting Edge."

"This is wild!" Sam commented.

Katie giggled, taking a bite of her vanilla sundae. "Really," she agreed. "Especially since I heard Stacy and Eva bragging to everyone that they personally know the Edge and are really good friends with her. That's such a joke!"

"I don't get it, R.Z.," Arizonna said, twirling the straw in his soda. "Why were you so upset at the skateboard shop? I mean, you should be happy that so many people are listening to you."

"Why?" I asked before I could stop myself. I didn't necessarily want them to know exactly how I felt. I mean, I couldn't even really explain it to myself. Besides, I'm not really good at telling people my feelings when it comes to personal things.

"Maybe Randy doesn't want people to just accept everything she says," Allison suggested. Sometimes I think Al knows me better than I know myself.

"Why not?" Jason asked. "I think it would be cool. Just think, you could get everyone to do practically anything just by suggesting it on the air."

"Really," Sam agreed. "You're practically a radio god, or something."

I could not believe what I was hearing. Those guys were hopeless. All I could do was bury my head in my hands.

"Oh, I get it," I heard Arizonna say. "Randy likes to question people and ideas."

"And she doesn't want people not to question her," Sabs added.

I looked up in surprise and smiled. I hadn't wanted to tell my best friends how I really felt because I wasn't sure they would understand. The kicker was that they already knew! Wild!

"I don't want people to assume that they should accept what I say without thinking about it, just because I'm on the radio," I explained. "Do you know what I mean?"

Sam gave me a curious look. "You mean, you want them to argue with you?" Sam asked.

"Well, not argue," I said. "It's just that all these people call up and ask me advice. I can't just hang up on them. And Spike thinks it's important that I put some of the calls on the air. He says it's good for me and for KTOP."

Sabs cupped her chin in her hands and asked, "So what are you going to do?" Then this horrified look came over her face. "Oh, my gosh! You're not thinking of telling Spike that you don't want to go on the air anymore, are you? Randy, you can't do that. We would die without the Cutting Edge!" Sabs can get really dramatic about things.

"I don't know what I'm going to do yet," I admitted. "I really like doing the show. Maybe I can work something else out."

Katie looked at me thoughtfully. "If you don't want to give advice on the air, then I guess we should just scrap the whole idea of saying something on your show about the dress code."

I noticed that Sabs's face kind of fell, but she didn't try to talk me out of it. It felt good that my friends were respecting my feelings, even though they obviously wanted me to speak out about the dress code on my show.

"What about the dress code?" Nick wanted to know. "I think it's totally bogus."

Allison scooped up the last of the ice cream sundae. "It doesn't seem fair," she agreed.

"But what can we do about it?" Jason asked, shrugging. "If Hansen wants a dress code, he's going to get a dress code."

"Not necessarily," Sabs said optimistically. She pulled a clipboard out of her book bag and handed it to Arizonna. "We have this petition going — about thirty kids have signed it already. And the next school board meeting is in two weeks. I'm definitely planning on going there to try to talk them out of the dress code."

Arizonna signed the petition and passed it over to Sam, in the other booth. "What is an extreme style, anyway?" he asked, frowning. "Sounds totally vague."

"I'm probably wearing one," I admitted, looking down at my clothes. I had on a black turtleneck with a zipper in the front, zebra print leggings, and black Pro-Keds. Sheck had paint-ed a white peace sign on both of my sneakers, and I wore a matching white peace pin on my black beret. I suppose in certain circles I might be called extreme. But, hey, what can I say?

"Well, I know my jeans count as sloppy," Billy said with a grin. He was right about that. His jeans were totally faded, the knees were ripped, and there was blue paint splattered all over them.

A completely horrified look came over Arizonna's face as he added, "This means I can't wear shorts to school, right?" To someone like Zone, I figured that must be like getting a life sentence in jail.

Jason nodded. "But girls can still wear miniskirts," he protested. "What's the difference?"

"I don't know," Katie admitted. "That's why I think the petition is a good idea. It might be the only way to make the school board see how unfair a dress code would be."

I didn't say anything while the rest of the guys signed the petition. I was glad that none of my friends mentioned anything more about my saying something on the air about the dress code. But I started thinking that maybe I should, anyway. I mean, people might listen to me. And I knew one thing for sure, I didn't want to get stuck wearing cardigan sweaters, argyle socks, and corduroys for the rest of my life. That would be a fate worse than death.

Chapter Seven

For the rest of the week, I kind of held back on the air when it came to giving advice. I don't know, I just did not want to be responsible for people doing stuff just because I said to.

By Monday night I could tell that Spike was getting a little annoyed. "It's good publicity, Ran," he kept telling me. "People love to hear the Edge's advice. You can't let your fans down." I took a couple of calls when he really insisted, but I have to say that I was not happy about it.

Finally, on Tuesday night, when we were walking to the high school from my house, Spike said, "I don't get it. It shouldn't be any big deal to talk to your fans, Ran. What gives?"

Instead of answering him, I said, "Spike, I've been thinking. I don't know if I want to give advice on the air anymore."

"What?" Spike asked. He ran his hand

through his wild brown hair, looking at me as if I had lost my mind. "Why not, Ran? You're a natural."

I let out a breath of air — I hadn't even realized I'd been holding it in. "First that guy Mike breaks up with his girlfriend, supposedly because of that rap song I played," I told him. "And then the other night I told what's-his-name that skateboards were cool, and when I went to the board shop, it was mobbed. Everyone wanted to buy a skateboard, because the Cutting Edge said that's the way to travel. Can't any of these bingo heads think for themselves?"

Spike laughed.

"This is not funny!" I exclaimed angrily.

"Easy, Ran," Spike told me, holding up his hands. "People don't do something just because you tell them to."

Putting my hands on my hips, I turned to glare at him. "Well, then how do you explain Mike's breakup and all those people who suddenly want to buy skateboards?" I demanded.

Spike shook his head in disbelief. "Randy, what do you think, that you're a mind alterer or something?" he asked, laughing. "That your words have a hypnotic effect on people? Take a reality break for a minute."

"What do you mean?" I asked, feeling a little uncertain.

"People don't do anything they don't want to, no matter how much you tell them to," Spike insisted. "Mike must have been thinking about breaking up with Jenny before you played that song."

Before I could say anything, Spike took a deep breath and went on. "And what's so bad about getting half the population of Acorn Falls to buy skateboards? I thought you loved skateboarding. You're always telling me I should try it. Give these guys some credit, you know? They have minds, too, Randy."

I opened my mouth but then quickly shut it. I am not usually the speechless type, but what could I say? Spike had a point. I wasn't a mind bender. I didn't have special powers or anything. And the kids in this town definitely weren't mindless.

Spike tapped my forehead with his finger. "You got it, right?" he asked, smiling at me.

"Yeah. I guess this whole D.J. thing went to my head," I admitted sheepishly.

"No problem," Spike replied. He grabbed my hand and gave it a quick squeeze. Then he started walking toward the high school again, pulling me along behind him. "That's why I'm the D.J. and you're just the assistant."

I laughed. "Thanks for clearing that up for me. I never would have figured it out on my own." Even though I was teasing him, I was kind of serious, too.

The two of us walked the rest of the way in silence. My mind was swirling with everything that Spike had said. He was right. I had been blowing the entire situation out of proportion.

So now I could get back to the other problem at hand — the dress code. Now that I felt more human, and less like a radio god, I felt as if I could actually do something about it.

I made it into the studio with all of Spike's albums and the stuff for my show five minutes before air time. Flipping the input switch back to the mike, Spike quickly slipped on the head-phones and started up his Grateful Dead intro while I cued his first commercial tape on the reel-to-reel. We were back in action, and it felt great!

An hour and a half later, Spike put his last

song on and stood up. "All yours, Ran," he said, handing me the headphones. "Go to it!"

Putting on the headphones, I checked the volume levels on the audio board, then set up my first two records.

"Yeah, mon!" I yelled into the mike as soon as Spike's song was over. "For those of you who don't know, that's Jamaican for get down! This is the Cutting Edge coming at you on KTOP 1350 AM. You're jamming to the Future Shock Show. And jamming is just what we're going to do. Here's Bob Marley!"

"Reggae, huh?" Spike asked as I flipped the selector from the mike to turntable one. "I like it."

"Thanks, mon," I replied, laughing. "There's something about reggae that makes me think about the sun. I feel better already."

After the Bob Marley tune was finished, I took a deep breath. I still wasn't sure what to do about this dress code business, so I decided the best thing would be to leave it up to my listeners.

"Party people in the house, pump it up!" I yelled into the mike. "How many out there go to Bradley Junior High? I want to know what you all think about this dress code they're proposing. Give a call and let the Edge in on it. Here's some more reggae to get you pumping!"

As soon as I started up turntable two, the phone rang. When I glanced over at Spike, I saw that there was a definite glint of admiration in his dark eyes.

"A poll about the dress code?" he asked, picking up the receiver and covering it with his hand for a second. "Way to go, Ran! I'll keep track for you." Then he put the receiver to his ear. "This is KTOP 1350 , you've got the Future Shock Show."

The phone must have rung seven or eight times during that one song. And then there were ten more calls during the next tune. I couldn't believe the response. Everyone was totally against the dress code and wanted to know what I thought.

"Time to go on record," Spike said, pointing at the mike. "Give some advice, babe."

This time I didn't even hesitate. As my third song ended, I switched the selector back to the mike. "We're jamming here at 1350 AM," I said. "All you folks at Bradley Junior High are coming in loud and clear. You're telling the Edge that the dress code isn't the way to go!"

Just then the phone rang again. Reaching over, I picked up the receiver myself and flipped it on the air. "KTOP 1350. This is the Future Shock Show. You're on the air!"

"Is this the Edge?" a guy asked.

"You've got her!" I replied. "Who's this?"

"My name's Jacob," he said.

I recognized this voice. Jacob Lowenstein is in seventh grade with me. He seems really conservative. Who would've thought that he'd be listening to my show? I thought he was totally into classical music. Not that there's anything wrong with that. "What can I do for you, Jacob?" I asked.

"I just wanted to say that I think a dress code would be unfair," Jacob said. "It discriminates against the guys. The girls at Bradley would still be able to wear miniskirts. Why can't we wear shorts?"

"You got me," I answered. "Sounds unfair to the Edge, too. Why should the guys pay the price in hot weather?

"Well, I think Bradley students have to make their voice heard," I said.

"What do you think we can do?" Jacob asked.

For the last week, I had been dreading it when people asked me that question. But now I was psyched to give advice. I gave Spike a thumbs-up, and he grinned. "Well, you know," I began. "I think that this skirts-shorts issue is pretty major. If you guys feel strongly about this, why don't you protest it?"

"But how?" Jacob wanted to know.

Suddenly the perfect idea came to me. The people in radio land were going to flip when they heard my suggestion.

"Why don't you wear a skirt to school?" I said into the receiver. I heard Spike groan in the corner, but I did my best to ignore him.

"A skirt?" Jacob asked, sounding really horrified.

"Bingo!" I exclaimed. "Time to make a statement! What is the difference between a skirt and shorts? Why should one be allowed and the other outlawed?"

"A skirt? You want me to wear a skirt?" Jacob repeated. He sounded as if he were about to faint or something.

"If you feel strongly, mon," I replied, "you've got to make a stand. Wear a skirt if you protest the Bradley Junior High dress code!"

I could hear Spike cracking up, and I'm sure all of radio land could as well. But I didn't care. I felt as if I was on to something here. This was a protest, but not really. No one would be breaking any rules, and our feelings would come across loud and clear. Mr. Hansen would know just how we felt about the dress code. What more could we ask for?

"Yeaaaahhhh, mon!" I yelled, switching the selector back to the mike after Jacob had hung up. "Here's another tune, folks."

I started up the turntable, hit the correct controls on the board, and looked over at Spike.

"What are you laughing about?" I asked him. He was doubled over in his chair and clutching his sides, he was laughing so hard. "Do you think protest is funny?"

It took Spike a few seconds to catch his breath. "A couple of hours ago you didn't even want to give advice about skateboarding, and now you're telling a whole school of guys to dress like girls . . ." he said, shaking his head. "Randy, you've come a long way!"

I grinned at him. "Let's just see if it works."

"It might," Spike said. "I've got six Bradley students on hold. Who do you want first?"

The response was overwhelming. Manny even came into the booth to check out what was happening. I saw him out of the corner of my eye as I watched the clock, waiting until exactly 8:40 and zero seconds to plug in my first commercial tape.

"Hey, Edge," he said after I'd flipped the selector on the audio board and sat back in my chair. "You've really started something here."

Uh-oh. I wondered if that meant I was going to get in some kind of trouble. Maybe asking guys to wear skirts was illegal to do on the air.

Turning toward Spike, Manny continued, "It's cool and all. Just make sure 1350 isn't held responsible, okay? I don't want to catch flak from the administration over at the junior high."

"No problem," Spike told him, coming over to stand behind me. As soon as the commercial tape was finished, he reached over my shoulder and grabbed the mike, gesturing for me to flip the selector on the board.

"Just to remind radio land, the opinions of the Cutting Edge do not necessarily reflect the views of this radio station," Spike said on the air. Then he pushed the mike toward me, turned, and walked back to his seat.

Manny nodded, gave us the thumbs-up sign, and left the room. As soon as Manny had walked into the room, I was sure we were going to have major problems. But now it seemed as if everything was cool.

All of a sudden, I heard Spike laugh. When I looked at him, he pointed at the mike.

"Oops!" I exclaimed, forgetting for a second that I was supposed to be on the air.

For the rest of the show, kids from Bradley Junior High kept calling, and I told them all the same thing — that the guys should wear skirts. I also figured that the girls should wear skirts, too, to show their support. I mean, it was the least we could do.

"I wonder how this will go over?" Spike mused after I had wrapped up the Future Shock Show and we were walking home. "I mean, you got people going. But guys wearing skirts? Do you think they'll go for it?"

I shrugged. "Most kids at Bradley are definitely not into this whole dress code thing," I said. "But I'm not sure how far guys are willing to go to protest it."

"I agree with that last guy who called in,

though," Spike said. "I mean, here these guys are going to be wearing skirts to school tomorrow and all, and the girls don't have to do anything."

"I know, it's not really fair," I replied as we turned onto Maple Street, the road we both live on. "But girls can wear skirts already. That's the whole point of it."

I could see Spike frown as we passed under a streetlight. "Why can't they do something else, then?" he asked.

A couple of callers had brought up the same point, and I hadn't been able to come up with a fair answer.

"The only other thing I object to is the extreme-styles thing. But that's really hard to protest," I pointed out, thinking aloud. "I mean, who has the right to judge what exactly is an extreme style? One teacher might think something was totally extreme, and the next teacher might not see anything unusual about it at all. So all the girls could come in their most extreme styles tomorrow, whatever they may be, and the administration might not think any of them are extreme."

Grinning at me, Spike added, "Then again,

you might go to school, dressed the same as usual, and get detention for being extreme."

"You got it!" I exclaimed. "It's totally absurd. Anyway, the best I could do was tell all the girls to wear skirts as a symbol of support."

"Only time will tell," Spike said as we stopped at the foot of my driveway. "Good luck, Ran."

"Catch ya on the upbeat, Spike," I said. I waved good-bye, then turned and ran up my driveway.

I had to get inside to call my friends. I couldn't wait to find out what they thought of my protest idea!

Chapter Eight

Arizonna calls Randy.

RANDY: Talk to me.

ARIZONNA: SKIRTS!?

RANDY: What?

ARIZONNA: Skirts? You want me to
                wear a skirt? No way!

Randy laughs.

ARIZONNA: I can't believe you're
                laughing about this! Do
                you know what you've
                done? I've got to wear a
                skirt to school! In public!
                A skirt!

RANDY: Zone, you told me you were
                opposed to the dress code,
                right?

ARIZONNA: So?

RANDY: Well, do you want to do
                something about it?

ARIZONNA: Sure. I get it, but I thought you said you weren't going to give advice anymore.

RANDY: I changed my mind. Besides, giving advice isn't the same thing as holding a gun to someone's head and forcing them to do something. It was just a suggestion, Zone. You don't have to do it.

ARIZONNA: Right.

RANDY: Don't get so uptight about it. Girls wear skirts all the time.

ARIZONNA: Well, maybe they've got better legs than I do.

RANDY: (*Laughing*) I guess we'll find out tomorrow.

ARIZONNA: I never said I was going to wear a skirt or anything. But, um, do you have one I could, like, borrow? Just in case.

RANDY: Not a problem. You want to stop by in the morning?

ARIZONNA: I guess so. If my surfing

	buddies could see me now!
RANDY:	They'd want your phone number?
ARIZONNA:	Very funny, Randy. Very funny. I've got to go. See you in the A.M.
RANDY:	*Ciao.*

Sabs calls Katie.

KATIE:	Campbell residence, Katie speaking.
SABRINA:	Katie! Did you hear Randy on the air tonight? All the guys at Bradley are going to wear skirts! I'm going to have to bring my camera to school tomorrow. It's going to be so funny.
KATIE:	Hi, Sabs. I did hear the Future Shock Show tonight. I can't believe she told all those guys to wear skirts! I don't think too many will, though.
SABRINA:	Why wouldn't they?
KATIE:	Well, do you think they will?

SABRINA: Arizonna told me that Randy's lending him a skirt. And Sam asked me if he could borrow three, for him, Nick, and Jason. Mark even asked me where he and his friends can get skirts to fit them. So even some eighth graders are going to do it. I wonder who else is going to wear one? Do you think Billy Dixon will wear one? I really can't picture that.

KATIE: Me either.

SABRINA: Anyway, everyone's going to meet here before school. I'm going to call Randy and tell her and Arizonna. You should definitely come, too. I think these guys are going to need all the help they can get.

KATIE: You're probably right about that.

SABRINA: I've got the best skirt for Sam to wear. He's going to die. I better make sure I've got film in my camera. I don't want to miss this.

KATIE: Don't forget, the Cutting Edge said all the girls should wear skirts, too. We've got to show support.

SABRINA: Oh, my gosh! What am I going to wear tomorrow? I better go through my closet now. You know, it's weird. My parents think this is a really good idea. I wonder why I'm surprised? Oh, well. So I'll see you tomorrow morning, right? We can just have breakfast here.

KATIE: All right. I'll see you tomorrow.

SABRINA: Bye.

Allison calls Randy.

MRS. ZAK: Hello?

ALLISON: Hi, Mrs. Za — I mean, Olivia. This is Allison Cloud. May I speak to Randy?

MRS. ZAK: Hi, Allison. How are you doing? Let me get the Cutting Edge for you.

RANDY: Hey, Al! What did you think? Do you think the reggae was too much? I mean, I know it's not played on a lot of the radio stations around here or anything.

ALLISON: I really liked it. It kind of made me feel as if I was sitting on a beach in the sun somewhere.

RANDY: Me too! That's wild. I should probably play it more often during the Minnesota winters. So what do you think about the skirt thing. Do you think it will work? I mean, Jacob Lowenstein called me up, and the idea just came to me.

ALLISON: It's definitely different. My father said it was an excellent example of civil disobedience. You know, because you're telling the guys to refuse to follow Mr. Hansen's rules and hope to get him to listen and not change the dress code.

RANDY: So do you think it will work?

ALLISON: I don't see why not. Do you think every guy will wear a skirt? It won't be as effective if only a couple of guys do.

RANDY: I only know of one guy so far. Arizonna called me and asked to borrow a skirt.

ALLISON: Billy called me.

RANDY: Billy? Billy Dixon? I can't believe
            it! He thinks it's a good idea?
            That's great.
ALLISON: He thinks it's really funny. Oh,
            Billy talked to Sam before. We're
            all meeting over at the Wellses' in
            the morning. I think the guys need
            a lot of support from each other
            when they walk to school.
RANDY: That's a good idea. I guess I'll call
            Sabs and see what's going on.
            Don't forget to wear a skirt tomor-
            row, Allison.
ALLISON: I won't.
RANDY: All right, so I'll catch you at Sabs's
            in the morning. *Ciao*.
ALLISON: Good night.

Randy calls Sabs.
SAM: Speak.
RANDY: Sam, you've really got to work on
            your phone manner. I thought I
            was pushing it, but *speak*!?
SAM: Oh, my gosh! It's the Cutting
            Edge! I'm talking to a real live
            celebrity! This is too much! I'm

going to faint!

RANDY: You and your sister are so much alike, it's unbelievable. Are you twins or something?

SAM: This skirt thing doesn't sound so bad, Randy. I think it's kind of a good idea. As long as every other guy in the entire school wears one, too. I don't want to look like a jerk. Do you think Mr. Hansen's going to listen to us now?

RANDY: I hope so. That's the whole point, right? Well, that and to show off your cute knees.

SAM: You're a riot, Ran. Let me get Sabs. Catch you tomorrow.

Sam calls Sabs to the phone.

SABS: Ran? You were great! What a totally outrageous idea. I love it! I can't wait to see Sam in a skirt.

RANDY: Sabs, this is a protest. We've got to take the guys seriously.

SABS: I know, I know. (*giggling*) It's just so funny. All the guys have been on the phone with Sam since you first talked to Jacob on the air. And

	when Sam's not on the phone, Mark's friends are calling.
RANDY:	The protest might work after all. I mean, lots of guys have to do it. Otherwise Mr. Hansen might just blow the whole thing off.
SABS:	Tomorrow's going to be history! You're coming over for breakfast, right? I already talked to Arizonna about it, and he said to tell you he'll meet you here.
RANDY:	Cool. I'll be there. I better motor. I've got some math problems to finish.
SABS:	Yeah. I've been working on those for like two hours and I've got seven more to go. Of course, I have been on the phone a lot and Sam was in my closet for a while.
RANDY:	I'll catch you in the A.M., Sabs.
SABS:	Bye.
RANDY:	*Ciao.*

Chapter Nine

"Sam, you're not going to wear those socks with that skirt, are you?" Sabs asked the next morning.

Sam, Nick, and Jason had just finished changing into their skirts down in Sam's room at the Wellses' house. Katie and I were waiting with Sabs up in Sabs's attic room. Since her room is very private, we thought the guys might feel a little more comfortable if they made their first appearance there.

"What are you talking about?" Sam asked, looking down at his feet.

I couldn't help it, I laughed. I mean, I knew I kept telling everyone that this was a protest and we had to take it seriously. But still. Sam was wearing a hot-pink-and-white-striped skirt over baggy grey sweats and black-and-red argyle socks.

"Where did you find that skirt, Sabs?" Katie

asked, holding a hand to her mouth. She was obviously about to laugh but trying not to.

Sabs giggled. "I haven't worn it in a while. In fact, I don't think I've ever worn it." she admitted.

"Where did you get it?" Sam asked, eyeing the skirt suspiciously.

"Grandma Wells," Sabs answered matter-of-factly.

Sam groaned. "I should have guessed," he said. "How come I didn't get one like Nick's? I mean, his is darker and longer. He doesn't look half as ridiculous as I do."

I looked at Nick's denim skirt, which he had on with a long-sleeved polo shirt. Sam was right. The skirt came down over Nick's knees. With his work boots, you could barely even see the long johns he had on underneath. He had definitely made out.

"I feel pretty stupid," Jason said, looking at his reflection in Sabs's mirror. He was wearing a long, narrow red knit skirt of Sabs's. "How do you guys walk in these things?" He took a big step and had to grab Sabs's dresser to keep from falling flat on his face.

Katie, Sabs, and I all giggled.

"Take smaller steps," Katie suggested.

Crossing his arms over his chest, Sam said firmly, "I'm not going outside without these sweats on. Don't even think about asking me to take them off. Besides, it's too cold out."

"Allison called a few minutes ago," Sabs interrupted Sam. "She and Billy are having breakfast at her house. Al said they'd be right over. In fact, you chickens, she said Billy was wearing his skirt over here."

"No way!" Sam exclaimed.

We all paused when we heard Mrs. Wells call up the stairs, "Pancakes are ready!"

Sabs took a couple of steps toward the door. "Come on," she urged. "I'm starving. Let's go eat."

The guys made Sabs, Katie, and me go down the stairs ahead of them and promise not to watch as they came down. We didn't want them to feel any more self-conscious than they already were, so we did what they asked.

"This is totally weird," Jason said as we all sat down at the Wellses' kitchen table. A pile of pancakes was on a tray, and they smelled great. "Sitting down in a skirt is totally different from when you're wearing pants."

Nick reached for the pancakes, piling four on his plate and smothering them with butter and syrup. "Man, this better work," he said. "I'd hate to think that we'd go through all of this and then not be able to wear shorts."

"Dudes!" Arizonna said, walking in the back door.

"Where have you been?" Nick asked. "We've been waiting for you!"

Arizonna joined the rest of us at the table. "You dudes are looking totally bodacious!" he said, serving himself some pancakes and digging in.

When we had finished eating, Jason said, "Let's hurry and get this over with before I chicken out." He turned to Arizonna. "Get your skirt on."

"Chill, dude," Arizonna replied. "I'm on my way. Did you bring me one, Edge?"

I pointed in the direction of the stairs. "It's in Sam's room," I told him.

"You can't miss it," Sam added. "Not too many other skirts in my room."

"Be back in a flash," Arizonna said and ran up the stairs. When he was gone, Katie turned to me and asked, "Do you think that skirt's too much, Randy? I mean, it's kind of wild."

"No way!" Sam said. "I won't wear pink."

"Maybe it is too much . . ." Sabs put in. She stopped talking as Zone's panicked voice called loudly from upstairs.

"NO! I can't wear this! No can do. I look ridiculous! It's not me. How do you walk in this? I can't get downstairs!"

We all looked at each other and cracked up.

"Come on, you can do it! The rest of us managed," Sam called up to him.

A few seconds later, Arizonna walked into the kitchen, stopping uncertainly just inside the doorway. For a long time, no one made a sound.

"Dude, that is hot!" Nick announced, breaking the silence. "I mean, very hot!"

Arizonna was wearing my leopard-print cotton miniskirt, which came down to right above his knees. Underneath it he had on his black Lycra surfing suit. He also had on black high-top sneakers, lime-green scrunchie socks, and a UCLA sweatshirt.

"I really don't know about this," he said slowly, looking down at his outfit. "I mean, I want to be able to wear shorts in May, but this might be going too far."

Sam grinned at him. "You haven't experienced a Minnesota summer," he said. "It's humid!"

"And Bradley has no air conditioning," Jason added. "Believe me, it'll be worth it."

Arizonna still looked unconvinced. I was beginning to think that he might back out when Billy and Allison walked into the kitchen.

"B.D.!" Sam exclaimed. "You made it!"

"How was your walk over here?" Jason wanted to know.

Billy looked down at his red pleated skirt, which he wore with a T-shirt and his worn leather bomber jacket. The skirt fell to right below his knees, and I could see that he was wearing long johns, too. Obviously, Billy and Nick had talked the night before. In my opinion, his high-top basketball sneakers and orange-and-black-striped tube socks really made the outfit perfect.

"Well, three guys asked for my phone number, and two of them wanted a date," Billy said, grinning as he answered Jason's question.

Even Sam and Arizonna cracked up when they heard that. We were all relieved to hear that Billy had already been outside in his skirt and survived. The guys suddenly all looked as if they felt better about the whole thing.

Katie suddenly snapped her fingers, saying, "I forgot to tell you guys. Flip, Michel, and Scottie all called me last night. The whole hockey team is meeting at Flip's house, and they're all wearing skirts."

"Fab!" I exclaimed. This thing was really taking off.

"Let me get a photo of this," Mrs. Wells said, walking into the kitchen. She had a camera in her hand. "You boys look terrific!"

"Mo-om!" Sam protested. "This is serious. It's not like we're going to a dance or something."

"I want to record this," Mrs. Wells insisted. "It's a moment for the scrapbook. You're going to want to remember when you stood up for your rights. I'm really proud of you boys."

Sam reddened a little. "Oh," he said. "When you put it that way . . ."

"Not a problem," I finished for him. I agreed with Mrs. Wells that the guys should feel proud of themselves.

After a quick couple of shots, I realized it was time to hit the road. "We'd better motor," I said, looking at my watch. "We don't want to be late."

"Oh, my gosh!" Sam exclaimed. "Then we'd get detention and we'd never be able to change out of these skirts!"

A worried look came over Nick's face as he pointed out, "Besides, I won't be able to run if we're late."

"Well," Jason said with a deep breath. "Here goes nothing!"

I crossed my fingers as we went outside. I really hoped this would work.

Chapter Ten

"Randy, you've got quite a following!" Sabs exclaimed, as I sat down behind her in homeroom later that morning. "I haven't seen a guy in pants yet."

I was in a great mood. It had been a big surprise to me to see that just about every single guy at Bradley had worn a skirt. And most of the girls had worn skirts, too, to show their support. Everyone was talking about how great Cutting Edge's idea was, and I could tell they really meant it.

"I have to say, Katie, that the hockey team looks great," Sabs commented.

"Yeah," I agreed. "I wonder how they got the flag girls to give up their skirts. I didn't think Stacy would ever part with hers."

"I wonder whose idea it was?" Sabs mused. "I didn't think those guys had it in them."

Katie didn't answer but just stood there

grinning.

"Don't tell me," I said, turning to her. "You suggested it to Scottie?"

Katie nodded and laughed "Well " she said, "you know they do everything like a team anyway. So I figured why not look like a team today, too?"

"Hi," Allison said as she came into the classroom and walked over to us. I noticed that she looked very serious. "I think Mr. Hansen's about to take some kind of action," she told us.

"What's going on?" I asked Al.

"I saw three members of the school board going into Mr. Hansen's office just a few minutes ago," she answered. "What else could they be talking about?"

I waggled my eyebrows up and down. "School lunches?" I joked.

Suddenly Sabs grabbed my arm and said excitedly, "Oh — I almost forgot! This is such a riot. Katie and I were by our locker before second period and we were talking about what a good idea this was and everything, and Stacy overheard us."

"Yeah?" I prompted. I had a feeling this was going to be good.

"And she came right up to us and said that the whole thing was really her idea!" Sabs finished.

"Not possible!" I exclaimed, surprised. But it figured. Stacy is like that. She can't stand it when anyone else gets more attention than she does.

Katie nodded. "Yeah. She said that she and the Cutting Edge are very close, and that last night, before the Future Shock Show, she called the Edge and suggested this whole plan."

I guess I should have been mad that Stacy was taking the credit for my idea. But the whole thing was so ridiculous that I couldn't help laughing.

"She's going to die when she finds out who the Cutting Edge really is," Sabs said with a grin. "I have to be there when she finds out. She's going to flip!"

The final bell rang, and Al and Katie went to their seats as the rest of the class filtered in — all wearing skirts. Before Ms. Staats could say anything, the loudspeaker crackled. Maybe it was my imagination, but I could have sworn the entire class sat forward in their seats — including me. This was one morning announcement I didn't want to miss.

"Will Rowena Zak please come to the principal's office?" Mr. Hansen's voice sounded out into the room. I cringed. I hate being called by my real name. A moment later the loudspeaker went dead.

"That's it?" someone asked. "What about our skirts?"

When I got to Mr. Hansen's office, I saw that what looked like the entire school board was already crowded in there.

"Rowena," Mr. Hansen said in his most no-nonsense tone of voice. "I called Mr. McManus first thing this morning as soon as I saw all the skirts."

Uh-oh, I thought. Maybe I am going to get in trouble.

"Now, I know that KTOP 1350 is in no way to blame for your actions," Mr. Hansen continued. "I just wanted to know who was behind this . . . er . . . protest, and if that someone went to my school."

A woman with a frizzy dyed-blond perm leaned forward. "So you're the Slicing Edge?" she asked me. "My kids love your show. I can't believe you're only in seventh grade."

The Slicing Edge? I tried not to laugh, since I didn't exactly think that would help our cause.

"Right," Mr. Hansen interrupted, obviously wanting to get back to the issue at hand. "I called all the members of the school board in this morning for an emergency meeting," he continued. "I felt we had some issues to address."

Someone snorted after Mr. Hansen said "dress." I could see that several members of the school board were trying to keep the corners of their mouths from turning up in a smile. Even Mr. Hansen had to fight to keep from laughing.

"Rowena, perhaps next time you have a problem with a proposed rule, I suggest that you come to see me before organizing a protest," the principal finally said.

Here it comes, I thought grimly. Here's where they give me detention for the rest of junior high.

Mr. Hansen cleared his throat. "But since you have taken such a strong stance on this issue," he went on, "I wanted to let you know personally that we've decided against the proposed dress code."

"Cool!" I exclaimed before I could stop myself. Then I tried to look serious. "That's great, Mr. Hansen."

"I don't want to keep you out of class any longer," he told me. "Now, go on back to class, and I'll make a general announcement about this."

"Thanks a lot, Mr. Hansen," I said with a grin.

A second later I was running down the hall back toward homeroom. I couldn't wait to see my friends. We had won! Our protest had worked! I wasn't going to have to wear cardigans and argyle socks after all. There was no dress code!

Chapter Eleven

Everyone was totally psyched that the dress code had been abolished before it was even started. Kids were talking about it all day long. And on the Future Shock Show that night, tons of people called to congratulate the Cutting Edge on her great idea. Not only that, but my identity as the Edge was still a secret, a fact I was kind of pleased about.

The rest of the week passed quickly between doing shows and going to school. It felt a little anticlimactic after the whole skirt thing, but good.

"It's your last show, Randy," Spike said as I walked into the station on Friday evening.

I nodded, suddenly feeling a little sad about leaving. "I'm going to miss being in the limelight," I admitted.

"You haven't been in the limelight," Spike pointed out, a mischievous twinkle in his eyes.

"This is radio. You could be in the dark, and it wouldn't make a difference."

Keeping my face serious, I asked him, "Did you ever think about comedy as a serious career option?"

"Well . . ." he began.

"Don't," I finished, grinning at him. "You'd starve."

"Oooh!" Spike exclaimed. "Copping an attitude already. Well, get to work. I need a lot of albums pulled tonight."

I didn't go into the record library right away, though. There was something I wanted to do first.

I cleared my throat, and pulled something out of my pocket. When Spike looked up, I gave it to him. It was a Grateful Dead button that I had found at The Opportunity Shop.

"This is for you," I told him, "just to let you know that I won't ever forget who gave me my big start." I pulled another pin out of my pocket and put it on the lapel of my jacket. "Really, thanks a lot for asking me to help out. This has been totally awesome." Spike just stood there staring back and forth from me to the pin.

Suddenly I started feeling self-conscious, so

I turned and walked into the record library.

I couldn't believe my air time was coming to an end. I had promised all my listeners in radio land that I would reveal my true identity, since a lot of people kept calling to ask me my real name.

I had taken extra time to prepare my last show. I wanted it to be kind of special. I know it seemed corny, but I wanted to do something to let my listeners know that I really appreciated them. I had thought a lot about what to play, and finally I came up with what I thought was a pretty good idea. I hoped my audience would like it.

I walked into the studio with the pile of Spike's and my albums just as Smooth was packing up to leave. He gave me a wide smile and held out his hand. "Edge, you are really something. I'm sorry to see you go, man."

"Hey, look at it this way. We can relax until Randy hits ninth grade," Spike put in. "Because after that, it's look out Acorn Falls!"

I was grinning as I shook Smooth's hand. "Count on it," I said.

"We'll be waiting. See you around," Smooth told me. Then he left the station.

Out of the corner of my eye, I saw through the studio window that three people had appeared in the adjoining lounge. I was busy helping Spike cue his records, so I didn't really look up.

"Hey, who's that?" Spike asked, sounding slightly annoyed. "We're about to go on the air."

Taking a closer look, I saw Sabs, Allison, and Katie standing in the lounge. They were all wearing black wigs that looked a lot like my hair.

"Hey, you guys!" I exclaimed, totally surprised. No one had told me that they were coming down to the studio. "What are you doing here? Why are you wearing those funky wigs?"

They all giggled.

"Well, you're a celebrity," Sabs joked. "We want to be just like you."

"You're our idol," Katie added with a grin. "People listen to you."

"The entire state of Minnesota is listening to your show," Al concluded.

"Wow!" Spike said, sounding impressed. "I didn't even recognize you guys with those wigs. Your own entourage, Randy. Pretty wild. And they even look like you."

"Yo, Spike!" I said, wanting to change the subject. "Fatal air, dude," I said, with a grin. "Fatal air."

"Oh, no!" he exclaimed, grabbing the mike and flipping the switch on the audio board.

As Spike launched into his show, I motioned to Al, Sabs, and Katie to come in. I put my fingers to my lips to tell them to keep quiet, since Spike was on the air. As they walked in, I grabbed their wigs off their heads. I just couldn't concentrate looking at three other people with my hair. It was too weird.

Then, before I knew it, Spike was putting in his last commercial tape. "It's all yours, Ran," he told me, standing up and handing me the headphones. "Let's hear it! Your last show!" He began applauding, and Sabs, Al, and Katie joined in.

I sat down and grinned at my friends. I was really glad that they were there. It definitely made my last night at KTOP more special.

"Party people!" I yelled as soon as I flipped on the mike. "Are you ready to rock? You're tuned in to the Cutting Edge on the Future

Shock Show. This is 1350, the station that jams! Let me hear you say yeah! Tonight's show is dedicated to my four best friends and the state of Minnesota."

Spike raised his eyebrows. I could tell that he didn't see how I could dedicate a show to a state. But he would find out soon enough.

"Minneapolis pumps!" I continued. "The Edge is coming at you with tunes from our own capital city, starting with that Minneapolis bad boy, Prince! This song is for all you dedicated KTOP listeners."

While the song played, I was busy concentrating on exactly how I should reveal myself to my radio audience. I had gotten a few calls already asking when the Edge was going to end the suspense.

"Hey, Randy, you've got to take this call. It's perfect!" Sabs said, interrupting my thoughts. Something in her voice made me turn and look at her. Sabs was waving the receiver back and forth, and she had this huge grin on her face.

Suddenly I was very curious. "What are you up to, Sabs?"

"This phone call," she replied. "You've got to take it on the air."

What was going on here? "But I thought we agreed that I should tell everyone who I really am now," I said.

"Just take the call, okay?" Sabs insisted. "It'll help. Really. Trust me."

Now I knew she was up to something. But she's one of my best friends, and I trust her. So I picked up the phone and flipped the right switches on the board. The call was on the air.

"Future Shock," I said into the receiver. "You've got the Cutting Edge, and you're on the — "

"Is this 1350?" a girl's voice interrupted me. I was positive I knew that voice, but I couldn't quite place it.

"You bet," I replied.

"Can I talk to the Cutting Edge, please?" the girl asked.

"You've got her, and you're on — "

"Well, this is Stacy Hansen," she said, cutting me off again.

I couldn't believe Stacy was calling me. I looked at Sabs. She had her hand over her mouth, trying to keep from laughing.

"You know, the principal's daughter at Bradley Junior High," Stacy continued before I could say anything. "Anyway, I told all these people that we were like really good friends and all, and I was wondering if you could dedicate something to me, one of your really good friends."

I could tell that Sabs, Katie, and Al were dying! They were all trying really hard not to totally crack up. Obviously Stacy had no idea she was on the air, though I had tried to tell her twice.

"Listen, Stacy," I began, trying again. "I think you should know that — "

"I just told a lot of people we were good friends, and I don't want them to know we're not," Stacy went on, totally unaware. "Listen, thanks a lot. I've got to go."

"Stacy," I said a little more loudly.

"Yes?" she said, sounding impatient.

"You're on the air!" I cried, grinning at Katie, Sabs, and Allison.

"What?!" Stacy sputtered. "But . . ."

"And I just want y'all out there in radio land to know that the Edge is dedicating this next tune to her best friends," I went on. "Sabrina Wells, Katie Campbell, and Allison Cloud."

I wished I could see Stacy's face. I felt kind of bad for her, but I really had tried to tell her. It was her own fault that she had said all that stuff on the air.

"But . . ." Stacy began again. "Oh, my gosh! That means . . . Oh, no! I don't believe it! The Cutting Edge must be Randy Zak. You're Randy!"

"That's right. What's up, Stace?" I asked. "Thanks for calling KTOP 1350 !" Then I hung up and switched on my next record.

"That was the best!" Sabs exclaimed. "I can't believe we got it on the air! Everyone heard it!"

I grinned at her. "Well, I just wanted everyone to know who my real friends are," I replied.

The rest of the show went by really quickly. When it was over, Sabs, Katie, and Al helped Spike and me put all the records away. This was it, the end of the Cutting Edge and the Future Shock Show.

When we were ready to leave the station, I hung behind for a second, looking around the studio. Being a D.J. had been great. I knew for sure that when I got to ninth grade, I would try to get my own show on KTOP 1350. But for right now, I couldn't wait to go to Fitzie's with my best friends.

Smiling to myself, I turned off the lights, and shut the station door behind me.

Look for these titles in the GIRL TALK series

1. WELCOME TO JUNIOR IIIGH!
Introducing the Girl Talk characters, Sabrina Wells, Katie Campbell, Randy Zak, and Allison Cloud. When our four heroines meet and have to plan the first junior high dance of the year, the results are hilarious.

2. FACE-OFF!
Katie Campbell is just plain fed up with being "perfect." But when she decides to join the boys' ice hockey team, she gets more than she bargained for.

3. THE NEW YOU
Allison Cloud's world turns upside down when she is chosen to model for *Belle* magazine with Stacy the Great!

4. REBEL, REBEL
Randy Zak is acting even stranger than usual. Could a visit from her cute New York friend have something to do with it?

5. IT'S ALL IN THE STARS
Sabrina gets even when she discovers that someone is playing a practical joke on her — and all her horoscopes are coming true.

6. THE GHOST OF EAGLE MOUNTAIN
The girls go on a weekend ski trip, only to discover that they're sleeping on the very spot where the Ghost of Eagle Mountain wanders!

THE WINNING TEAM
⭐13 It's a fight to the finish when Sabrina and Sam run against Stacy the great and Eva Malone for president and vice-president of the seventh grade!

EARTH ALERT!
⭐14 Allison, Katie, Sabrina, and Randy try to convince Bradley junior high to turn the annual seventh grade fun fair into a fair to save the Earth!

ON THE AIR
⭐15 Randy lands the after-school job of her dreams, as the host of a one-hour radio program. But she's not so sure being a celebrity is all that great!

HERE COMES THE BRIDE
⭐16 There's going to be a wedding in Acorn Falls! When Katie's mom announces plans to remarry, Katie learns that she's also getting a step-brother.

STAR QUALITY
⭐17 When Sabrina's favorite game show comes to Acorn Falls, she's determined to get on the show, *and* get her friends to be part of her act.

KEEPING THE BEAT
⭐18 Randy's band Iron Wombat is more popular than ever after winning the Battle of the Bands. But Randy's excitement turns sour when the band is booked for Stacy the great's birthday bash!

LOOK FOR THE GIRL TALK SERIES!
IN A STORE NEAR YOU!

TALK BACK!

TELL US WHAT YOU THINK ABOUT GIRL TALK

Name _____

Address _____

City _____ State _____ Zip _____

Birthday Day _____ Mo. _____ Year _____

Telephone Number (___) _____

1) On a scale of 1 (The Pits) to 5 (The Max),
how would you rate Girl Talk?   Circle One:

          1   2   3   4   5

2) What do you like most about Girl Talk?

___Characters___Situations___Telephone Talk

Other _____

3) Who is your favorite character? Circle One:

     Sabrina   Katie   Randy

      Allison   Stacy   Other

4) Who is your least favorite character?

_____

5) What do you want to read about in Girl Talk?

_____

_____

Send completed form to :
Western Publishing Company, Inc.
1220 Mound Avenue Mail Station #85
Racine, Wisconsin 53404